The Boy Who Grew Flowers

For my brother Wally, because you were
there to show me that what makes us
different is what makes us wonderful.
— J. W.

To Kathleen, my mother — S. A.

Barefoot Books
2067 Massachusetts Avenue
Cambridge, MA 02140

Graphic design by Jemima Lumley, Bristol
Reproduction by B & P International, Hong Kong
Printed in China on 100% acid-free paper
This book was typeset in Celestia Antiqua
The illustrations were prepared in acrylics on board

ISBN 978-1-84686-749-1

Library of Congress Cataloging-in-Publication Data
is available under LCCN 2004028584
1 3 5 7 9 8 6 4 2

The Boy Who Grew Flowers

Written by Jen Wojtowicz

Illustrated by Steve Adams

Barefoot Books
Step inside a story

Rink Bowagon was a boy from the deep country.
He lived out past where the blacktop road
became a dirt road, and the dirt road
petered out into a little footpath.

The path wound through the ancient trees
of a wild forest, hopped Black Bear Creek,
headed all the way up Lonesome Mountain,
made a right-hand turn and ran smack
into the Bowagons' door.

The Bowagons were the only folks
who lived on Lonesome Mountain.
The townspeople argued as to whether it
was because they were such strange folk that
they lived there, or whether it was because they
lived there that they were such strange folk.
However, everyone agreed that the Bowagon
clan was a hotbed of strange and exotic talents.
Rink's Uncle Dud liked to tame rattlesnakes,
and his brothers and cousins
were all shape-shifters.

But Rink himself had the most special
talent of all: during the full moon he sprouted
flowers all over his body. It was a
beautiful sight, and they were the prettiest,
sweetest-smelling and longest-lasting
blossoms you ever saw.

Some folks might stay home sick in bed if
they happened to sprout — but not Rink.
Every morning following a full moon, his mama
would gently clip the flowers from her boy
and off he would go to school.

Now, Rink liked school, at least he liked
the thinking and reading part.
But he was shy and quiet and different
from the other children, so the teacher gave
him a seat at the back of the room
and did not bother with him.
As for the children, they had all
heard rumors about Rink's strange
relatives, so they stayed at a safe
distance from him.

One day Angelina Quiz came along,
a girl whose family was in the
ballroom dancing business and
had just moved from Tuscaloosa.
She was what some would call
a plain girl. She had an easy
manner, a luminous smile, and her
right leg was shorter than her
left by an inch. She always wore
a flower behind her right ear.
Rink liked her straight away.

So did everyone else. Angelina was always surrounded by friends. Rink observed her from a distance.

"She is forthright and honest, yet always kind," he thought.

He also admired the flowers she wore behind her ear, a different one every day, and all of them as lovely as she.

As for Angelina Quiz, she soon wondered about this quiet boy who sat alone at the back of the class. So she asked the other children about him.

"His Uncle Dud has a pet rattlesnake called Fat Lucy and she sleeps on the end of his bed!" hissed Fuster Shrimp.

"And his mother uses a bowling bag for a purse!" giggled Shirleyanne Smeeth.

"And his granny was raised by wolves!" snickered Gertrude Prugg.

Angelina did not laugh. "Why won't anyone talk to him?" she asked. The others fell silent. The question rattled in their minds.

One afternoon, the teacher announced that
the school dance would be held that Saturday
night at the church hall. Several of her classmates
asked Angelina to go, but she smiled
bravely and shook her head.

Dance

Saturday Night

"I wouldn't be much of a dancing partner," she laughed.

Rink was struck by the wistful note he heard in her voice. "She comes from a dancing family," he thought. "I bet she loves music. I bet she'd really like to go to that dance."

The minute the teacher's back was turned, Rink slipped out the door. No one noticed except Angelina, who glanced back at his empty chair every now and then. She marveled at how his absence could take the shine off such a pretty, sunny day.

When Rink reached his home high on
Lonesome Mountain, he went straight to
his Uncle Dud's room. He rummaged under
the bed until he came up with several feet of
Fat Lucy's shucked-off skin.

Next, he dug through his mama's bowling bag
until he found a needle and spool of silk
thread. Then, in the tumbledown shed off
the kitchen, he turned up an old leather
mule saddle.

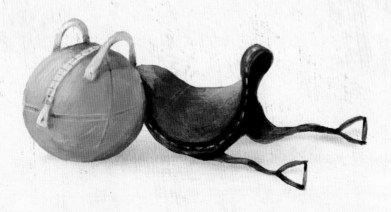

Fig.22

a' b' c' d'

b^2 c^2 d^2

A a b c d e f g h B

F

B

Fig 9

E

S

H

G S'

$$(x_1, x_2, \ldots, x_n)$$

$$\sqrt{x_1^2 + x_2^2 + x_3^2}$$

Rink sat down and cleared his mind.
He thought intently about Angelina's feet.
He pictured their shape and size and
the inch of space between her right foot
and the floor. Then he cut and
stitched and glued. He worked right
through from Thursday afternoon
until Saturday morning.

When Rink was finally done, there on the table stood the loveliest pair of snakeskin slippers that have ever been seen this side of Black Bear Creek. The sole of the right slipper was one inch thicker than the left, so that Angelina could stand true and straight and tall. Rink imagined her dancing. He thought that thought so long, and the feeling deep inside him was so pleasant, that even though the full moon had not yet risen, he sprouted a bunch of wild pink roses from the top of his head.

That afternoon, Rink followed the footpath
down through the forest, across
Black Bear Creek, along the dirt road,
on to the blacktop road and up the hill.
Halfway up the hill, he opened a small gate
and walked up the little path that led
right to Angelina's front porch.

Angelina was helping her mama sew up a fancy
new tango dress. The whole house was quiet,
and every little snip of the scissors made a sad
little tweak in her heart. She thought
about Rink and how she had missed him
at school all day Friday.

When Angelina heard a knock at the door,
her heart flipped. There stood Rink, with a
bunch of wild pink roses in his left hand and
a pair of snakeskin slippers in his right.

"These are for you," he said as he offered
the slippers to her. "If you wear these, you'll
dance just fine."

Angelina wriggled her bare toes into the slippers
then and there. For the first time in her life,
she felt herself stand up straight. She took
one step, then another, and then she did a little
practice dance step. Angelina looked
at Rink with delight.

"Will you be my dancing partner?" she asked.
"I don't know how to do that kind of dancing,"
said Rink shyly.
"I'll teach you!" cried Angelina. "I've watched my family
so many times I know all of the steps by heart!"
She took his hand, and they danced
together down the path.

After the dance, Rink walked Angelina
home. They stopped on the way and sat
under an old buttonball tree. Angelina told
Rink about her family, and he told
her about his.

Then, with a pounding heart, he revealed
to her the fact that he sprouted
flowers all over himself during the full moon.
Angelina smiled with delight. Then she bent
down and showed Rink where the flower she
wore grew right out from behind her ear!

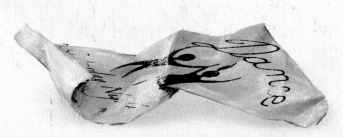

From that day on, Angelina Quiz
and Rink Bowagon were fast friends.
Angelina wore her snakeskin slippers
every day. And when the slippers wore
out, Rink made her another pair.
He has been making all of her shoes for
twenty-five years now. The two of them
have their own house up on
Lonesome Mountain — only these
days, it's called Sweet Blossom Hill.
Gardening is how Angelina and Rink earn
their living. Actually, it's a family business.
You see, every one of their seven children
was born with a green thumb.